BABY SHARK

Doo Doo Doo Doo Doo Doo

Art by John John Bajet

SCHOLASTIC

Watch out for a dance guide at the end of the story!

This edition published in the UK in 2019 by Scholastic Children's Books
Euston House, 24 Eversholt Street, London NW1 1DB
A division of Scholastic Ltd
www.scholastic.co.uk
London – New York – Toronto – Sydney – Auckland – Mexico City – New Delhi – Hong Kong

First published in 2018 by Cartwheel Books, an imprint of Scholastic Inc., U.S.A.
Copyright © Scholastic Inc., 2018
Adapted from the song, "Baby Shark".

ISBN 978 140719 582 7
All rights reserved.
Printed in Italy

3 5 7 9 8 6 4 2

A long, long time ago, there lived a . . .

Baby Shark, doo doo doo doo doo doo.
Baby Shark, doo doo doo doo doo doo.

Baby Shark, doo doo doo doo doo doo.
BABY SHARK!

Mama Shark, doo doo doo doo doo doo.
Mama Shark, doo doo doo doo doo doo.

Mama Shark, doo doo doo doo doo doo.
MAMA SHARK!

Daddy Shark, doo doo doo doo doo doo.
Daddy Shark, doo doo doo doo doo doo.

Daddy Shark, doo doo doo doo doo doo.
DADDY SHARK!

Great White Shark, doo doo doo doo doo doo.
Great White Shark, doo doo doo doo doo doo.
Great White Shark, doo doo doo doo doo doo.

Grandma Shark, doo doo doo doo doo doo.
Grandma Shark, doo doo doo doo doo doo.

Grandma Shark, doo doo doo doo doo doo.
GRANDMA SHARK!

Here they come! Doo doo doo doo doo doo.
Here they come! Doo doo doo doo doo doo.

Here they come! Doo doo doo doo doo doo.
HERE THEY COME!

Shark attack! Doo doo doo doo doo doo.
Shark attack! Doo doo doo doo doo doo.

Shark attack! Doo doo doo doo doo doo. SHARK ATTACK!

Swim real fast! Doo doo doo doo doo doo.
Swim real fast! Doo doo doo doo doo doo.

Swim real fast! Doo doo doo doo doo doo.
SWIM REAL FAST!

Safe and sound! Doo doo doo doo doo doo.
Safe and sound! Doo doo doo doo doo doo.

Safe and sound! Doo doo doo doo doo doo.

SAFE AND SOUND!

That's the end! Doo doo doo doo doo doo.
That's the end! Doo doo doo doo doo doo.
That's the end! Doo doo doo doo doo doo.

THAT'S THE END!

BABY SHARK DANCE!

BABY SHARK!
Pinch two fingers together like a shark mouth.

MAMA SHARK!
Snap both hands together like a bigger shark mouth.

DADDY SHARK!
Snap arms together like an even bigger shark mouth.

GREAT WHITE SHARK!
Snap one arm and one leg together like the biggest shark mouth.

GRANDMA SHARK!
Snap two closed hands or fists together like a toothless shark mouth.

HERE THEY COME!
Bring two hands together in a point on top of the head like a shark fin.

SHARK ATTACK!
Spin arms around the head like a whirlpool.

SWIM REAL FAST!
Wave arms back and forth in a swimming motion.

SAFE AND SOUND!
Use the back of one arm to wipe your brow.

THAT'S THE END!
Do a wiggle dance with fingers pointing up.